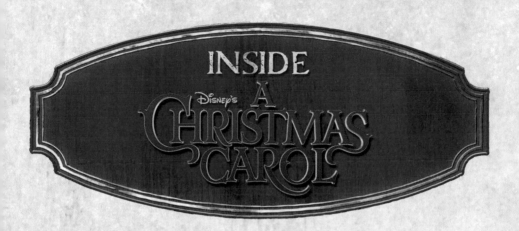

INSIDE
Disney's A CHRISTMAS CAROL

Based on the classic story by Charles Dickens
Based on the screenplay by Robert Zemeckis
Produced by Steve Starkey, Robert Zemeckis, Jack Rapke
Directed by Robert Zemeckis

Disney PRESS
New York

Copyright © 2009 Disney/IMD

All rights reserved. Published by Disney Press, an imprint of Disney Book Group.

No part of this book may be reproduced or transmitted in any form or by any means,
electronic or mechanical, including photocopying, recording, or by any information
storage and retrieval system, without written permission from the publisher.

For information address Disney Press, 114 Fifth Avenue, New York, New York 10011-5690.

Printed in the United States of America

First Edition

1 3 5 7 9 10 8 6 4 2

Library of Congress Catalog Card Number on file.

ISBN 978-1-4231-2212-8

For more Disney Press fun
visit www.disneybooks.com
Disney.com/ChristmasCarol

In 1843, Charles Dickens created
something amazing. He blended ghost stories
and Christmas stories together with fantastic
results. This newest version of *A Christmas Carol*
is a revolutionary combination of imagination,
talent, and visual effects. All the art you'll see
in this book was used to help create the world
of *Disney's A Christmas Carol*, and it will shine a
new light on just how amazing this story truly
can be.

From the cobblestoned streets of London
to the stars high above them, every inch
of the world of *Disney's A Christmas Carol* was
made with amazing detail. In this dark and
spooky place, we are introduced to Ebenezer
Scrooge, a bent and bitter old man who cares
for only one thing: money.

But Ebenezer Scrooge isn't the only
character in this story. Bob Cratchit is
a warm and caring person who works in
the shadow of Mr. Scrooge.

Even though the pay is horrible and Mr. Scrooge is a mean old man, Bob is a cheerful father who loves Christmas! Bob, supported by his loving family, works hard for Mr. Scrooge.

The night before Christmas, Scrooge is visited by the ghost of his former business partner, Jacob Marley. Marley's ghost has been forced to wander the earth, trapped by chains symbolizing the greed that ruled Marley when he was alive.

Marley's ghost warns Scrooge that he must change the way he lives his life, or he will share Marley's fate. And he famously warns Scrooge of the three ghosts that will visit on Christmas Eve.

The Ghost of Christmas Past is the first
to arrive. The ghost's head, which flickers
like the flame of a candle, lights the road
into Scrooge's history. Scrooge's cold heart
begins to thaw when he is reminded of his
childhood. It has been a long time since he
thought of the family and friends that made
him happy when he was younger.

From the cold streets of London, the
Ghost of Christmas Past brings us to the
warm and loving parts of Scrooge's past.
Both Scrooge's sister, Fan, and his first love,
Belle, show us that even a man as closed off
as Scrooge once had love in his heart.

A colorful part of *A Christmas Carol* occurs when the Ghost of Christmas Past takes Scrooge back to the place where he had his first job. The sight of Mr. Fezziwig makes Scrooge smile.

Mr. Fezziwig's endless energy and the love he has for his workers shows Scrooge that giving back to the people in your life isn't a bad thing. He finally begins to realize that his treatment of Bob Cratchit should change.

This feeling continues when Scrooge
encounters a face he hasn't seen in a
long time: his own! When Scrooge sees
his younger self enjoying Mr. Fezziwig's
Christmas party, he is forced to remember
the time in his past when friends and loved
ones meant more to him than money.

The Ghost of Christmas Past makes it clear that Scrooge is to blame for the man he has become. Scrooge is forced to watch from the outside as his love of money turns him away from those who cared about him. Finally, when Scrooge can't take any more, he tries to extinguish the flame on the ghost's head, with explosive results!

The Ghost of Christmas Present is Scrooge's next visitor. A friendly giant who seems to enjoy whisking Scrooge all across London, the Ghost of Christmas Present embodies everything that is comforting and warm about Christmas.

The Ghost appears, surrounded by a
mighty feast, and joy radiates from his form.
By comparison, the Ghost of Christmas Past
was a quiet being.

Through his travels with the Ghost of Christmas Present, Scrooge sees people enjoying Christmas, no matter how rich or poor they may be. And though the Ghost of Christmas Present only exists for as long as Christmas Day, Scrooge gets to see the spirit age. By the end of their journey, the ghost appears as an old man, a symbol of how every day should be lived to the fullest.

Scrooge is left alone once more, and
even though all he wants to do is go home,
there is one more spirit coming for him.

A large, imposing, and speechless figure,
Scrooge knows from the second he lays eyes
on the spirit what the Ghost of Christmas Yet
to Come represents—Death!

And while the Ghost of Christmas Yet to Come is a frightening spirit, it is also the one that brings out the best in Scrooge. After seeing the life he has led and its effects on those around him as well as on himself, he promises to change. Scrooge shows that it's never to late to apologize, and it's never too late to live a good life.

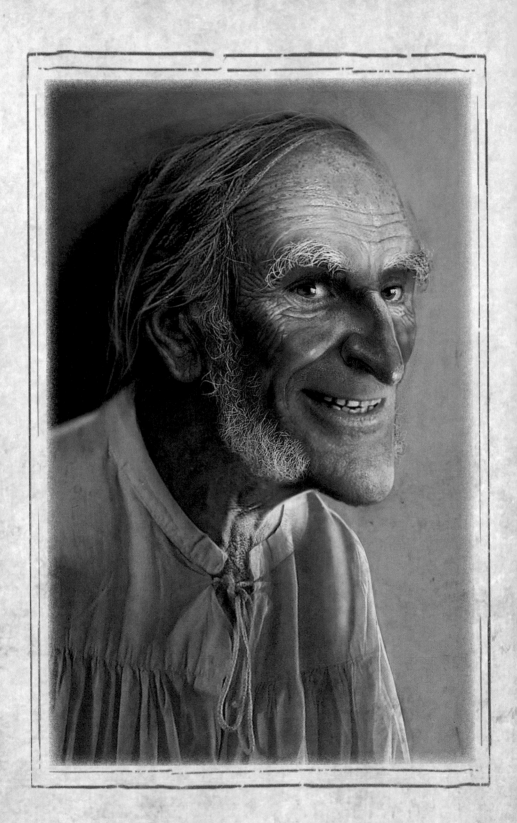

At the end of his fantastic voyage, Scrooge's life has new meaning. We see a revitalized man with a spring in his step and a gleam in his eye. He immediately makes good on his promise to be a better man and begins helping those around him.

There is no one Scrooge abused
more than Bob Cratchit, and thankfully,
there is no one Scrooge helps more than
Bob. The Cratchit family, and especially
Bob's ill son Tiny Tim, are taken under
Scrooge's wing. He promises to make sure
Tiny Tim gets the care he needs, and at the
same time he helps the Cratchits have the
Christmas celebration they deserve. It's
a brighter day in all of London now that
Ebenezer Scrooge has changed his ways.

A Christmas Carol is a story that has sparked people's imaginations for well over a century. The 2009 film brings this amazing tale to new heights. As a result of Scrooge's willingness to change his ways and be a better person, people who see this film will be given the chance to look at their own lives and to see that treating others with kindness and respect will always be an important part of a life worth living.